P9-CLR-211

Grover's
10 Terrific Ways
to Help Our
Wonderful World

By Anna Ross
Illustrated by Tom Leigh

"Sesame Workshop"®, "Sesame Street"®, and associated characters, trademarks, and design elements are owned and licensed by Sesame Workshop. ©1992, 2008 Sesame Workshop. All Rights Reserved.

Dalmatian Press, LLC, 2008. All rights reserved.
Published by Dalmatian Press, LLC, 2008. The DALMATIAN PRESS name and logo are trademarks of Dalmatian Press, LLC, Franklin, Tennessee 37067. No part of this book may be reproduced or copied in any form without written permission from the copyright owner.

Printed in the U.S.A.
ISBN: 1-40375-012-2

08 09 10 11 NGS 10 9 8 7 6 5 4 3 2 1
17378 Sesame Street 8x8 Storybook: Grover's 10 Terrific Ways to Help Our Wonderful World

Hello, everybodee! Is this not beau-ti-ful? The world is such a wonderful place! The world is our home. The mountains and deserts, the rivers and lakes belong to all of us.

The world gives us everything we need to live—food to eat and water to drink and air to breathe!

The world also gives us snow,
sunshine, and rain!

The world takes good care of us, so
we must all take care of the world.
Oh, I know we can do it!

I, Grover, your cute, furry World Ranger, will now tell you ten terrific ways to help our wonderful world.

Elmo and Herry are planting a tree.

3 RE-USE THINGS RATHER THAN THROWING THEM AWAY.

Ernie plants his seeds in empty milk cartons. When the plants are big enough, he'll put them in a window box.

Bert sorts his brown buttons and shiny paperclips into an old egg carton.

Grouches are great at making
treasures out of trash!

4 GIVE USED AND OUT-GROWN CLOTHES, BOOKS OR TOYS TO SOMEONE WHO MIGHT WANT THEM.

When Snuffy's sweaters get too small for him,
he gives them to his little sister, Alice.

When Elmo learns to ride a two-wheeler,
he will give his tricycle to Baby Natasha.

5 CHOOSE THINGS THAT CAN BE USED OVER AND OVER AGAIN.

Big Bird carries his own shopping bag to the store instead of getting a new bag every time.

Prairie Dawn takes her lunch in a lunchbox instead of in a plastic bag.

Instead of throwing broken things
away and buying new things,
first see if they can be repaired.

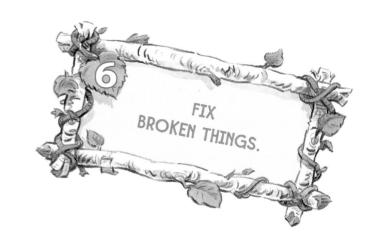

6

FIX
BROKEN THINGS.

7

DO NOT
WASTE WATER.
USE JUST WHAT YOU NEED.

Bert turns off the
faucet instead of
running the water
while he brushes
his teeth.

Ernie keeps water in the refrigerator instead of letting the tap run until the water gets cold.

DO NOT
WASTE ENERGY.

Betty Lou uses cool water instead
of warm water whenever she can.
It takes energy to heat water.

Cookie Monster closes the refrigerator
door quickly so the cold air can't get
out. It also takes energy to cool air!

Telly turns off the TV
when his show
is over.

The Count turns off the lights
when he leaves a room.

RECYCLE PAPER, BOTTLES, PLASTICS, AND CANS.

Recycling means using old things to make new things. When we recycle things instead of throwing them away, there is a lot less trash in the world.

RECYCLE HERE

GLASS   CANS

I, World Ranger Grover, and my friends take bottles and cans to places where they can be recycled.

We tie up newspapers in bundles and put them out at the curb so the recycling truck can pick them up. Old paper can be recycled into new paper!

Oh, I am so happy!
There is so much we can do to help our wonderful world.

1. Respect and be kind to all living things.
2. Take care of plants in your neighborhood.
3. Re-use things rather than throwing them away.
4. Give used and outgrown clothes, books or toys to someone who might want them.
5. Choose things that can be used over and over again.
6. Fix broken things.
7. Do not waste water. Use just what you need.
8. Do not waste energy.
9. Always put trash where it belongs.
10. Recycle paper, bottles, plastics, and cans.